The Kingdom
The Palace
Burth
Mermaid's Cove
Crestwood

of Wrenly
Flatfrost
Primlox
Bogburp
The Mainland
Hobsgrove

The Kingdom of Wrenly

5

Adventures in Flatfrost

By Jordan Quinn

Illustrated by Robert McPhillips

LITTLE SIMON
New York London Toronto Sydney New Delhi

If you purchased this book without a cover, you should be aware that this book is stolen property. It was reported as "unsold and destroyed" to the publisher, and neither the author nor the publisher has received any payment for this "stripped book."

This book is a work of fiction. Any references to historical events, real people, or real places are used fictitiously. Other names, characters, places, and events are products of the author's imagination, and any resemblance to actual events or places or persons, living or dead, is entirely coincidental.

LITTLE SIMON
An imprint of Simon & Schuster Children's Publishing Division
1230 Avenue of the Americas, New York, New York 10020
First Little Simon paperback edition October 2014

Manufactured in the United States of America 0417 MTN
6 8 10 9 7 5
Library of Congress Cataloging-in-Publication Data
Quinn, Jordan.
Adventures in Flatfrost / by Jordan Quinn ; illustrated by Robert McPhillips.
— First edition.
pages cm. — (The kingdom of Wrenly ; 5)
Summary: Mischief-makers Prince Lucas; his best friend, Clara; and Ruskin the scarlet dragon learn to respect the hard work of others when they are sent to Flatfrost to fetch more ice from the giants who live there.
ISBN 978-1-4814-1388-6 (pbk) — ISBN 978-1-4814-1389-3 (hc)
ISBN 978-1-4814-1390-9 (eBook)
[1. Princes—Fiction. 2. Dragons—Fiction. 3. Giants—Fiction. 4. Behavior—Fiction.
5. Conduct of life—Fiction. 6. Punishment—Fiction.]
I. McPhillips, Robert, illustrator. II. Title.
PZ7.Q31945Ad 2014 [Fic]—dc23
2013048044

CONTENTS

CHAPTER 1

Hide-and-Seek

Whoosh! Flames swirled from Ruskin's mouth and torched a giant block of ice. It hissed and melted into a puddle. Prince Lucas and his best friend, Clara, scurried behind another stack of ice and crouched.

The friends had been playing hide-and-seek in the larder all afternoon. Stacks and stacks of enormous ice blocks filled the room, which was located beneath the kitchen in the castle cellar. The ice kept the royal food cold. The larder was also the perfect place to play a chilly round of hide-and-seek. This had become their favorite game.

Lucas and Clara poked their heads above a stack of

ice blocks and waggled their tongues at Ruskin. The dragon scampered toward them. *Whoosh!* He blasted another fireball at a huge wall of ice blocks. The wall melted, but there was no sign of Lucas or Clara. They had already found a new hiding spot.

Ruskin splashed across the cellar floor in search of his friends.

Clang! Clang! Clang! The royal cook stood on the cellar stairs, banging together pans. Ruskin yelped and hid behind a stone column. Lucas and Clara stayed out of sight behind the last tower of ice.

"Stop the madness!" shouted the cook. "You'll spoil my food!"

Lucas and Clara peeked at the royal cook from their hiding place.

The cook had ruddy cheeks, bushy black eyebrows, and a round middle. He wore a starched white hat with many pleats. Each pleat stood for an outstanding recipe and was awarded by the king and queen of Wrenly.

The cook's real name was Berwick, but everyone called him Cook.

Lucas had never heard Cook sound so angry.

"Maybe if we stay hidden, he'll go away," whispered Lucas.

Clara nodded and squeezed her eyes shut.

"I know you're in here!" Cook shouted.

Drip. Drip. Drip. Water dripped from the thawing food onto the floor. Lucas and Clara stayed perfectly still.

"You'd better surrender, Prince

Lucas!" said Cook. "Or I'll report you and your naughty dragon to your father, the king!"

"What should we do?" whispered Clara.

"I guess we'd better face up to Cook," Lucas whispered back.

Lucas and Clara slowly stood up and came out from behind the ice blocks. They squeezed sideways between a leg of lamb and a side of beef that hung from the rafters. Cook glared at the children.

"Uh-oh," whispered Lucas. "Cook looks like he's about to explode."

CHAPTER 2

Spoiled

"My meats! My poultry! My pies and custards! All my food is going to go bad!" cried Cook. "How can I make the royal meals with spoiled food?"

Lucas had to admit, he hadn't thought about the food spoiling. It had been fun to hide behind the ice blocks, and Ruskin had just as much fun melting the ice with his fiery breath. This had been the best game of hide-and-seek they'd ever played.

"Can't we just order more ice?" asked Lucas as he, Clara, and Ruskin followed Cook upstairs to the kitchen.

Cook wheeled around on the steps and stared at Lucas.

"No, we *cannot!*" shouted Cook. "We had our ice delivery yesterday morning. The giants deliver ice from Flatfrost only once a month!"

Cook shook his head. "I don't know which is more spoiled," he went on, "my food—or *you!*"

Lucas hung his head and Ruskin cowered behind his master.

"Do you children know what the giants have to do to bring ice to the palace?"

Lucas and Clara shook their heads. They had no idea, but they had a feeling they were about to find out.

"Each and every block of ice is

hand-cut from one of Flatfrost's high mountain lakes. It's very hard work. The giants haul the harvested ice down the mountain by horse-drawn sleds. At the bottom of the mountain, the ice is transferred onto wagons. Then the ice is brought over rocky dirt roads to the castle."

"Oh," Lucas said.

He and Clara had occasionally seen the wagonloads of ice arrive at the castle, but they'd never really given it much thought.

Then Cook shook a fat finger in

the children's faces. "Ice is a luxury!" he declared. "It involves hard work—something you two know very little about."

Lucas and Clara nodded. What else could they do? They felt terrible that they had upset Cook.

Cook squeezed his pudgy hands into fists. "Just wait until your father hears about this!" he ranted. "He will *not* be pleased."

And with that, Cook marched out of the kitchen to find the king.

CHAPTER 3

Penalties

"I'd better go," said Clara.

"Okay," Lucas said. "I'll see you later."

Clara hurried out the kitchen door and down the steps.

Lucas turned to Ruskin.

"Get ready for another lecture," said Lucas.

Ruskin whimpered. The prince stroked his dragon's swept-back horns. The two of them had gotten into a lot of trouble lately, especially Ruskin. Ruskin had developed a fire-breathing problem. He breathed fire like most children like to blow bubbles. Poor Ruskin. He hadn't meant to cause any harm, but the damage had begun to add up.

Ruskin had scorched the castle walls inside and out. He had torched Queen Tasha's favorite tapestry of the royal family crest. He had charbroiled the royal swing set—not to mention the royal teeter-totter and

tree fort. Not only that, Ruskin had set the royal apple orchard on fire. The king had lost four of his prized apple trees. And now Ruskin had melted almost all the ice in the larder.

Lucas heard footsteps in the hallway. Stefan, one of the king's men, entered the kitchen.

"Prince Lucas, the king will see you in the library," he said.

Normally, Stefan didn't address Lucas in such a formal way. *This is not a good sign,* thought Lucas.

"Come on, Ruskin," he said to his dragon. "Let's go."

"Not so fast," said Stefan. "Ruskin must go straight to his lair."

Then Stefan tied a rope around Ruskin's neck and led him away. Ruskin squawked and whined.

"It'll be okay, buddy," said Lucas as he walked into the hallway.

Lucas wasn't sure if it would be okay or not, but he would soon find out. He entered the library. The king and queen sat next to the fireplace

in gilded chairs. His father had his arms folded. He didn't look happy.

"Son," began King Caleb.

Lucas hated it when his father began with the word "son." It rarely ended well.

"This time, you and your mischievous dragon have gone too far," said the king. "You have destroyed Cook's ice and possibly all the food in the larder. Tell me, how could you be so thoughtless?"

Lucas looked at his boots.

"It has become clear that the castle is no place for a dragon," the king went on. "I never should have allowed it."

King Caleb then looked to Queen Tasha for support. The queen nodded for him to go on.

"You have given me no choice,"

said the king. "Ruskin will have to return to Crestwood for proper training."

Lucas lifted his head and stared at his father in disbelief.

"No, Father! Please don't take Ruskin away!" he cried. "I promise I'll be better about training him."

The king's face did not soften. "I'm afraid you are *both* in need of training," he declared. "As punishment for your reckless behavior, you and Ruskin will go to Flatfrost first thing in the morning."

"Flatfrost!" cried Lucas. "But why?"

"Because I want you to apologize

to the giants," said the king.

"For what?" questioned Lucas.

"You have caused them more work," said the king. "Therefore you will apologize, and you will also help harvest more ice for Cook."

"But, Father!" protested Lucas.

"No buts," said the king. "You must learn to fix your own mistakes. And when you return, Ruskin will go to Crestwood for training."

Lucas frowned at his father. Then he ran to his room and slammed his door as hard as he could.

CHAPTER 4

In a Pickle

Lucas punched his pillow. He didn't want to go to Flatfrost—and, even worse, what if Ruskin had to go to Crestwood for a long time? *How will I live without him?* Lucas wondered. His dragon had become his faithful companion. Lucas loved to spend time with Clara, too, but she was often busy. Clara had school most days, and then she had to make

bread deliveries with her father.

But Ruskin was always there for Lucas. Lucas buried his face in his pillow. *What if Ruskin can't be trained?* he thought. *What if he never comes back?* Lucas stared at the ceiling. A few minutes later he was called for dinner, but he didn't feel like eating. He yawned, and soon he fell fast asleep.

In the morning, sun streamed through the turret windows and Lucas's eyes popped wide open. His mother sat on the edge of the bed.

"I brought hot chocolate," she said, setting the mug down.

Lucas sat up and rubbed his eyes. Then he remembered his father's punishment.

“Oh, Mother!” wailed Lucas. “Do I really have to go to Flatfrost?”

“Yes,” said the queen as she gently stroked Lucas’s forehead with her fingertips. “You and Ruskin must learn to respect people and their work.”

Flatfrost was in the mountains, where it snowed year round. Lucas had passed by Flatfrost on horse-back, but he'd never traveled into the mountains.

"Clara will also go with you," his mother went on. "Her parents would like her to apologize to the giants too."

"How long will we have to be there?" asked Lucas.

"Until the ice is cut."

"And how long will that take?"

"A few days," the queen said.

"I don't want to go," Lucas complained. "I don't want to leave you and Father for that long."

"I don't want you to go either. But it will be good for you. You may even like it."

Lucas sniffled, and his mother handed him a handkerchief.

"Right now you need to get dressed," she said, patting him on the shoulder. "Then you may join us for breakfast before you go."

Lucas flopped back down on his pillow and moaned.

"Come on now," said the queen, ruffling his hair. Then she got up and left the room.

Well, at least Clara and Ruskin will be with me, he thought.

CHAPTER 5

Farewell

"Time to go, Prince Lucas," said Stefan. "Miss Clara has arrived."

Lucas pushed out his chair from the breakfast table and followed Stefan to the front hall. Clara was already examining the huge pile of traveling clothes that were left out for them: lovely fur coats and fur hats, along with fur-lined gloves and boots. Lucas also found woolen undergarments, a shirt, trousers, socks, and underpants.

"This is what you'll wear on the trip," Stefan said.

Clara tried to imagine being cold enough to wear fur coats.

"Please put on the woolen undergarments and the boots for the first part of the journey," Stefan continued. "We'll put on our outer clothes when we get to the mountains."

After Lucas and Clara got changed, they helped Stefan load the wagon with supplies. Cook had made several enormous loaves of bread to take to the giants. Once the bread had been loaded and one

of the king's men had gotten Ruskin from his lair, they climbed aboard the horse-drawn wagon.

The large wagon was led by two horses. Stefan said they would need the extra room to carry the ice back

to the castle. Then the king and queen and Clara's mother saw them off.

"Be a good boy," said his mother with a warm smile.

"Do some good thinking," said the king.

"Mind your manners," said Anna, Clara's mother.

Lucas and Clara waved good-bye.

I can't believe our parents are sending us away, thought Lucas.

CHAPTER 6

Snowball!

The wagon bumped along the dirt road to Flatfrost. Clara and Ruskin rode in the back, and Lucas sat up front with Stefan.

Stefan patted the prince on the back. "This trip will be good for you," he said.

"What makes you think so?" mumbled Lucas.

"Because it will help you grow

into a better person," Stefan replied.

"But what about Ruskin?" asked Lucas.

"Ruskin will grow too," said Stefan.

"And what if he doesn't? Then he'll have to go to Crestwood for training."

"He'll come back," said Stefan.

"But what if he can't be trained?" questioned Lucas. "Ruskin can be stubborn. He doesn't always listen to commands."

"Tell me, how many dragons have you trained?" asked Stefan.

"None."

"Exactly," said Stefan. "But André and Grom have trained dozens of dragons."

"But not scarlet dragons," Lucas protested.

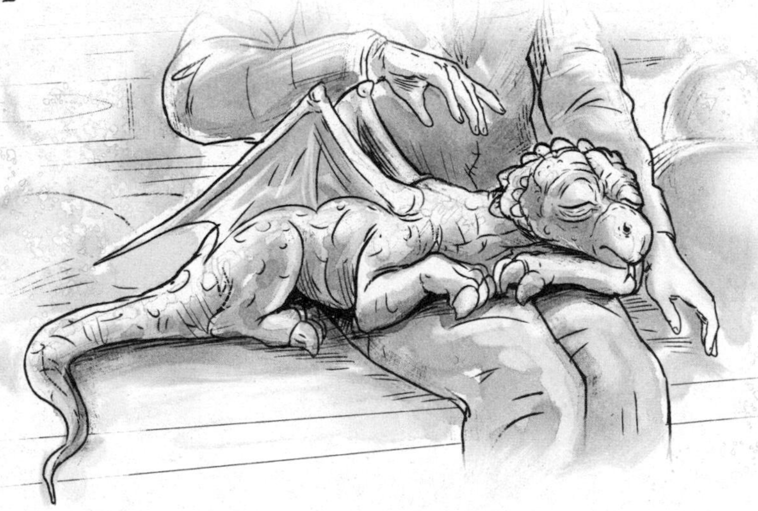

"True," Stefan said. "But they'll do their best, and you must do your best to correct your own mistakes."

"I know, I know," Lucas said.

Soon they arrived at a stable at the bottom of a mountain. Snowflakes drifted from the gray sky. They changed into their warm fur clothes and transferred the supplies from the wagon

to a sled. Stefan cracked a whip, and the horses began to head up the mountain. Lucas and Clara watched snowflakes land on their mittens.

"They look like frosty jewels," noted Clara. "I wish I could take them home with me."

"Me too," said Lucas.

Ruskin squawked and tried to catch the snowflakes on his forked tongue. Lucas and Clara laughed.

They began to feel a little better about being sent away.

In the late afternoon Lucas spotted a cave in the distance. Then he noticed something roll from the mouth of the cave toward them. It began to pick up speed.

"What's that?" shouted Lucas.

Clara and Stefan looked where Lucas was pointing.

"Oh my!" Stefan cried. "It's a great ball of snow!"

"And it's getting bigger!" warned Clara.

The snowball thundered down the mountain. Lucas and Clara put up their arms like a shield.

"LOOK OUT!" Stefan shouted.

CHAPTER 7

Gumlock

Whoosh! Ruskin blew a great ball of fire at the oncoming snowball. It melted instantly. At the same time, Stefan jerked the reins. The horses whinnied and came to a stop.

"That was close!" said Lucas.

"A little *too* close," agreed Stefan.

"Good boy, Ruskin!" Clara said, patting his head. "You saved us from getting smashed."

They sat quietly for a moment and heard laughter. Lucas saw three giant children standing at the mouth of the cave. The children wore shaggy fur clothes and had long, knotted hair. They laughed and pointed in the direction of the snowball. Then two grown giants with stern faces appeared beside the children. Suddenly the giant children became very serious.

Lucas had seen giants before, but he'd never met one in person. His father had told him the giants of Wrenly were not to be feared. They were very strong beings with troll-like faces, but they were

also ice harvesters, fishermen, and ice sculptors for the kingdom. Still, Lucas shuddered at their great size.

The grown-up giants began to walk toward the sled. The children skipped along close behind.

"Hello, Stefan," said the biggest giant, looking down at them. His wife stood nearby him with their

three children. The oldest boy looked about Lucas and Clara's age. The middle child was a girl, and the youngest was a boy.

"We're so sorry about the snowball. The children were playing a game, and it got away from them," the biggest giant went on. "What brings you to the mountains of Flatfrost?"

"Hello, Gumlock," said Stefan, who knew the giant from his ice deliveries. "We're here on a mission."

"What kind of mission?" asked Gumlock.

"The children and the young dragon have gotten into some trouble," explained Stefan.

Lucas squirmed in his seat, and his face grew hot.

"These must be the young trouble-makers," observed Gumlock.

Stefan nodded and introduced the culprits.

"This is Lucas, prince of Wrenly; his best friend, Clara Gills; and Ruskin, the prince's scarlet dragon."

"And what's their crime?"

The giant children stared at Lucas, Clara, and Ruskin. They couldn't wait to hear what they had

done wrong. Lucas scowled. *This is so embarrassing,* he thought.

"The young dragon has unthinkingly destroyed some of the king's belongings," Stefan answered, "and the children have been in on it."

"I see," Gumlock said.

"Yesterday the dragon melted the ice in the larder during a game of hide-and-seek," explained Stefan.

The giant children giggled. The mother giant put a finger to her lips and shushed her children.

"The king has sent Lucas and Clara to help cut more ice."

Gumlock stroked his beard thoughtfully.

"And what about the dragon?" he asked.

"The dragon will be sent to Crestwood for training when we return," said Stefan.

Gumlock nodded understandingly. "Cutting ice is very hard work," he said. "Even for giants."

He studied Lucas and Clara for a moment.

"The children may

come with us to the lake in the morning," he said, "and perhaps we can help the dragon as well."

"Thank you," said Stefan.

Then Gumlock helped Stefan unload the sled. Lucas, Clara, and Ruskin followed the mother giant and children into the cave. Lucas and Clara looked around at the high ceiling and gigantic furniture. They had never felt so small.

CHAPTER 8

Hard Labor

The prince and Clara slept on beds of straw and woke to the smell of baked bread and mulled cider. They followed the delicious smells into the cave kitchen. The giant children, Tublock, Thea, and Farfalee, showed Lucas and Clara to a pair of very tall chairs. They had to climb ladders to get to their seats.

"Father, may I harvest ice too?"

asked Tublock, the oldest giant child.

Gumlock smiled at his son's offer. "Not this time," he said. "I want you and your younger sister and brother to take Ruskin to the obstacle course for training."

Tublock clapped his hands. "Oh,

I'd love to do that!" he cried.

Lucas and Clara wanted to go with the children, but they knew they had to go with Gumlock. It was part of their punishment.

After breakfast Lucas and Clara helped load a sled with pickaxes and shovels. Another giant, a cousin, named Huffie, joined them, and off they slid toward the lake. The sled glided into a wide-open snowfield.

Windswept snowdrifts stretched out before them.

"I feel like I'm on top of the clouds!" Clara exclaimed.

"Me too," said Lucas.

A snow-covered lake sparkled in the morning light. Gumlock handed Lucas and Clara shovels. Then they scooped the fresh snow off the ice. When they had cleared a large patch of snow, Gumlock marked a checker-board pattern on the ice. Then Gumlock and Huffie chopped at the ice with pickaxes. Lucas and Clara cleared more snow.

"This is tiring," said Lucas.

"You said it," agreed Clara.

"This is called hard labor," Gumlock said. "And you two are doing very well for your first time."

This made Lucas and Clara feel better about what they were doing. They began to appreciate what the giants did for the castle. No wonder Cook had been so angry about the melted ice. Cutting ice blocks wasn't easy.

As the sun went down, Gumlock and Huffie loaded the blocks of ice onto the sled. Then they covered them with hay. The hay would keep the next layer of ice blocks from sticking.

Back at the cave, Lucas and Clara devoured bowls of stew served in giant thimbles.

"How'd Ruskin do in training today?" asked Lucas.

"Very well. He's beginning to master his fire breathing," said Tublock.

"How long will it take?" Clara asked.

"If a dragon is willing," said Tublock, "it only takes a couple of days to get the hang of it."

"Is that true?" questioned Lucas. "When I try to train Ruskin, he never listens."

Tublock grinned. "We've found a way to get him to listen," he said.

Thea and Farfalee giggled.

"How?" Lucas asked.

"We'll show you tomorrow," said Tublock. "My father said you could come with us to the obstacle course."

"We'd love that," said Lucas.

Then Lucas and Clara had to get ready for bed. They washed, climbed up their ladders, and hit the hay.

CHAPTER 9

Obstacle Course

Lucas, Clara, Tublock, Thea, and Farfalee tromped over a snow-packed trail to the obstacle course. Tublock pulled a sled with supplies behind him. Ruskin bounded ahead of the others. When they got to the top of the hill, the children sledded down onto a snowfield.

Spread out before them were tunnels, sled chutes, and climbing structures—all made from snow! Ice targets stretched across the landscape. Carved snowmen stood in rows, holding clubs, battle-axes, and war hammers. There was even a maze of ice, and a snow village.

"Did you make all this?" asked Lucas.

"We did over many months," said Tublock proudly. "This is what we do for fun in Flatfrost."

"It's a snowy playground!" Lucas exclaimed.

"It's amazing," Clara declared.

"Let's get to work," Tublock said. "We haven't much time before you'll have to return to the castle."

He pulled a big wooden bucket from the sled and set it on the ground in front of the targets.

"I hold in this bucket the secret to dragon training," said Tublock.

Clara and Lucas looked in the bucket.

"Fish?" questioned Lucas.

"Yes, your dragon *loves* fish!" Thea exclaimed. "He'll do anything for it."

"Watch this," said Tublock.

He threw Ruskin a fish. Then he gave Ruskin a hand signal. Ruskin leaped toward the ice targets and shot a fireball through each one.

"Target practice will help Ruskin gain control over his fire breathing," Tublock said.

Farfalee threw a fish to Ruskin as they moved to the next obstacle.

"This one will be much harder," said Tublock. "Ruskin must disarm the army of snowmen without melting them."

Tublock gave him a signal. Ruskin raced toward the snowmen.

He disarmed twelve snowmen and melted three. Lucas and Clara watched in amazement.

"He's improving," Tublock said. "Yesterday he melted six snowmen."

Then they moved on to the ice maze.

"Ruskin must enter the maze and find his way to the other exit," explained Tublock. "He must control his frustration—and his fire—when he hits a dead end."

Tublock signaled and Ruskin bounded into the maze. The

children walked around the outside of the maze toward the exit. They could hear the dragon galloping and panting up and down the pathways.

They clapped and cheered Ruskin on. Ruskin only scorched two walls before he found the exit. They practiced until the sun went down.

At dinner, Gumlock asked, "How did Ruskin do today?"

"He's mastered his basic fire-breathing skills," said Tublock. "He is now able to control his fire."

"The king will be pleased," said Gumlock.

Lucas nodded in agreement. "Now maybe I won't get in trouble all the time," he said.

"Me neither!" agreed Clara.

Everyone laughed.

A few days later, Stefan hitched the team of horses back to the sled. The time had come to go home.

"Please come back and visit," said Tublock.

"We will," Lucas and Clara promised.

Then the prince turned to Gumlock. "Thank you," he said. "I'm sorry we caused you so much trouble."

"I'm sorry too," Clara said.

"Well, did you learn something?" asked Gumlock.

"We sure did," said Lucas. "Now we'll be more thoughtful of other people's belongings."

"Somehow I think Ruskin will be more thoughtful too," said Gumlock.

"Definitely," Lucas said.

Then they waved good-bye and headed for home.

CHAPTER 10

Showstopper!

Stefan parked the wagon by the kitchen entrance. Lucas and Clara jumped to the ground.

"May we go?" asked Lucas.

Stefan smiled. "Yes, you may go," he answered.

"See you tomorrow!" called Clara as she ran down the lane toward home.

"Bye!" Lucas said. Then he put

Ruskin on a leash—just in case—and they ran up the stone steps two at a time to the kitchen. He stopped when he saw Cook.

"We've brought you more ice!" Lucas declared.

"Well done!" said Cook.

"You're right. Harvesting ice is hard work," Lucas said. "And I'm so sorry for all the trouble we caused."

Cook dropped his spoon into his mixing bowl and gave Lucas a hug.

"Apology accepted," he said.

Then Lucas headed to the royal library to see his mother and father.

"Welcome home, son," said King Caleb.

"We missed you!" Queen Tasha exclaimed.

Lucas told his parents all about their adventures in Flatfrost.

"I'm glad to hear that Ruskin has improved," said the king.

"He has," Lucas said. "Does he still have to go to Crestwood?"

"Not if his fire breathing is really under control," said the king.

"Can I set up an obstacle course and prove it?" Lucas asked.

"That would be splendid!" replied the queen.

Lucas smiled. "You are hereby invited to the garden balcony at four o'clock for a show of skills."

The prince invited Clara's family to come over too. Then Lucas and Clara called upon the king's men to help set up an obstacle course. They ordered archery targets, suits of armor, and weaponry from the armory.

The children asked Cook to make tea and cakes for their guests. Then they ran to the balcony and set up chairs and tables. The balcony had a perfect view of the obstacle course below. The king's men had already set up the targets and were putting

the suits of armor into formation.

The guests arrived at four o'clock. Lucas ran to the lair and got Ruskin. Then he grabbed a bucket of fish from the kitchen.

Everything was ready.

Stefan blew the royal trumpet and then announced the

show. "Your majesties and special guests," he cried, "I now present Ruskin the scarlet dragon!"

The king and queen and Clara's parents clapped their hands. Then Lucas threw a fish to Ruskin and gave him a signal.

Ruskin dashed toward the targets and blew a perfectly round hole in each one. Everyone clapped and whistled. Lucas showed Ruskin a fish and gave him another signal. The dragon disarmed the knights'

armor and didn't burn a single suit. Everyone on the balcony jumped to their feet and cheered.

"Well done!" cried the king.

"Bravo!" Cook yelled.

Then, as Ruskin enjoyed his fish, Lucas looked up at the balcony.

"Father, does Ruskin still have to be sent to Crestwood? Or can he stay?"

The king stood by the balcony railing. "Son," said the king with a smile, "Ruskin may stay."

Hear ye! Hear ye!
Presenting the next book from
The Kingdom of Wrenly!
Here's a sneak peek!

"So, guess what?" said Clara as she tried to ignore Bella's watchful eye.

"What?" asked Lucas.

"I have an idea for our next adventure."

Lucas's eyes widened. He loved it when Clara got ideas. "What is it?"

"My teacher said we have to research a place in Wrenly that we haven't been before," Clara explained.

Excerpt from *Beneath the Stone Forest*

"Where *haven't* you been?" Lucas asked.

"The Stone Forest," said Clara. "Have you ever traveled there?"

"I've only seen it from the road."

"Same here," said Clara.

Then Bella huffed. "Why would anyone want to go there?" she questioned. "Isn't it just a bunch of crummy old towers and creepy dark tunnels?"

Clara almost said, *Who asked you?* But she stopped herself. If Bella didn't want to go to the Stone Forest, then Lucas wouldn't be able to go either. *Hmm,* thought Clara. *How can I make this adventure sound like something that Bella would want to go on?* She took a good look at the princess. Then she noticed the lovely gemstone hanging in the middle of princess's forehead. This gave Clara an idea.

"Bella, did you know the most beautiful jewels in the kingdom come from the Stone Forest?" she asked. "Those creepy underground tunnels are just bursting with precious gems."

Bella's eyes lit up. "Precious gems?"

"Sparkling jewels everywhere!"

"I *love* jewelry!" Bella exclaimed. "When do we leave?"

Excerpt from *Beneath the Stone Forest*

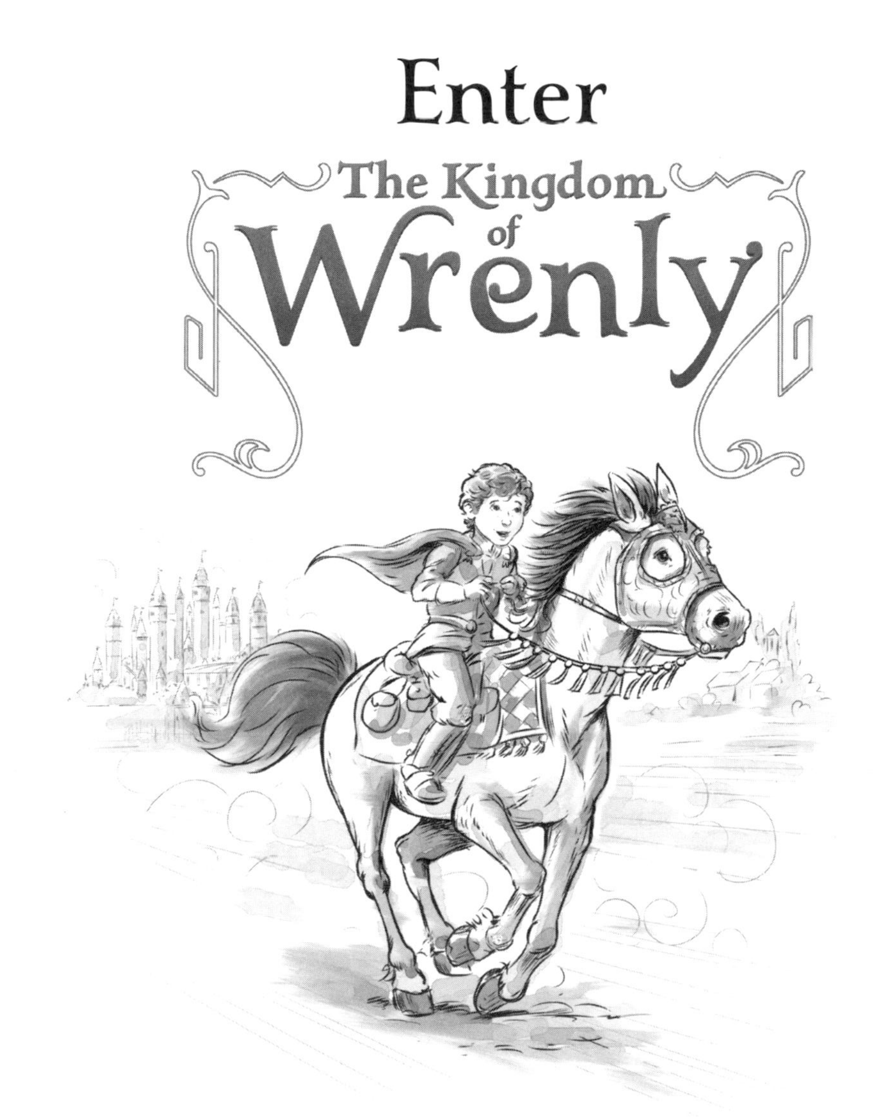
Enter
The Kingdom of Wrenly

After thoughtlessly melting all the ice in the castle, Prince Lucas and Ruskin must face the consequences. The king sends them to Flatfrost to fetch more ice from the giants who live there. High in the snowy mountains, Lucas, Clara, and Ruskin find help among a group of unlikely friends, and learn what hard work goes into cutting the ice that so easily melts.

With easy-to-read language and illustrations on almost every page, The Kingdom of Wrenly chapter books are perfect for beginning readers.

Look for more books about
THE KINGDOM OF WRENLY
at your favorite store!

Meet the au... rator
g...
KIDS.Sim... ter.co

ISBN 978-1-4814-1388-6 $5.99 U.S./$6.99 Can.
50599
9 781481 413886

EBOOK EDITION ALSO AVAILABLE

LITTLE SIMON · Simon & Schuster, New York · Cover design by Laura Roode · Ages 5-9